To all my Indian family, especially Mommy and Pappa

Hi
there!

First published in 2016 by Child's Play (International) Ltd
Ashworth Road, Bridgemead, Swindon SN5 7YD, UK

Published in USA by Child's Play Inc
250 Minot Avenue, Auburn, Maine 04210

Distributed in Australia by Child's Play Australia Pty Ltd
Unit 10/20 Narabang Way, Belrose, Sydney, NSW 2085

ISBN 978-1-84643-929-2
CLP030616CPL07169292

Printed in Shenzhen, China

1 3 5 7 9 10 8 6 4 2

A catalogue record of this book
is available from the British Library

www.childs-play.com

That's NOT
how you do it!

Ariane Hofmann-Maniyar

Lucy knew how to do everything.

She knew how to eat with a spoon and fork.

She knew how to play the xylophone.

Lucy knew how to do gymnastics...

and how to build a tall tower.

She knew how to paint an elephant just right...

and how to fold perfect stars.

In fact, if you didn't know how to do something, you came to Lucy for help.

Everything was fine,
until the day Toshi arrived.

He did not know how to eat
with a spoon and fork.

That's NOT how
you do it!

His music was strange.

Toshi's gymnastics were all wrong...

and his tower wasn't half as good as Lucy's.

He did not know how to draw
an elephant like she did.

And when he started to make
a paper star that was ALL wrong,
Lucy couldn't keep quiet any longer.

That's NOT how you do it!

Hey Lucy! This is for you!

This is lovely,
Toshi.
What is it?

It's a
paper crane!

Will you show me
how to make one?

Yes! And will you
show me how to
make a star like this?

They had so much fun that they made
a whole flock of paper cranes...

and a night sky full of paper stars.